ELVEN WARRIOR

Laura Shenton

ELVEN WARRIOR

Laura Shenton

Iridescent Toad Publishing

Iridescent Toad Publishing.

Cover by JV Arts.

First edition. ISBN 978-1-913779-12-2

*Extra special thanks to Des M. Astor
for helping me bring this book to life.*

Chapter One

The storm raged relentlessly, sheets of rain lashing against the lone figure kneeling in the field. Kora, a young elven woman barely into her twenties, trembled as the cold seeped into her bones. Her pale skin prickled with goosebumps, and her soaked clothes clung to her lithe frame as she knelt on the sodden grass. Above, dark clouds roiled and churned, seething with fury.

With shaking hands, she gingerly traced the constellation of bruises blooming across her arms. Each touch sent a jolt of pain through her body, a stark reminder of the betrayal she'd just endured. Her azure eyes, usually bright and welcoming, now glowed with an intensity that matched the storm's ferocity.

As a deafening crack of thunder tore through the sky, Kora threw back her head, her scream of raw frustration swallowed by the roaring tempest. Gritting her teeth, she glared upwards at the ominous funnel forming in the clouds, its dark, swirling mass a mirror to the turmoil within her.

Seeming to sense her distress, several winged creatures soared overhead. Their iridescent bodies, roughly the shape and size of horses, glistened in the rain as they danced through the storm, drinking in the lightning and revelling in the downpour. Kora watched them with a mixture of awe and envy, a part of her longing for their freedom and power. If only she could command such beasts, she mused bitterly. Then perhaps she could return to the town of Northfox and demand the answers that she had so cruelly been denied.

Restless energy coursed through her veins, prompting Kora to stand. She laced her fingers together in front of her, squeezing them so tightly that her knuckles turned white. She began to tremble, her movements growing increasingly erratic as her mind raced, replaying the events that had led her to this moment of exile.

"I defended them from monsters," she muttered, her voice shaking with indignation. "And this is how they repay me?"

The injustice of it threatened to overwhelm her. Kora had once thought the townsfolk were her friends. They had shared stories over ale at the tavern and exchanged cheerful greetings in the bustling streets. When trouble brewed, however, their trust in her faltered and quickly turned to suspicion and accusation.

Now, alone and banished from the town she had always thought of as home, a pang of regret shot through Kora as she realised that her bow and quiver of arrows, her primary weaponry, still lay in the cottage she'd been forced to abandon. How many other treasured possessions had she left behind? Would the townsfolk, in their misguided fear, loot her home? The thought made her stomach clench painfully.

Suddenly, a movement in Kora's peripheral vision caught her attention. She turned, heart racing, to see the imposing silhouette of a griffin prowling at the edge of the nearby forest. Its amber eyes glowed in the darkness, fixed on something hidden among the trees. Kora held her breath, willing herself to keep still. After a moment, she let out a shaky sigh of relief. If the creature had noticed her, it showed no interest.

As the storm raged on, Kora's analytical mind refused to relent. She found herself dissecting the day's events over and over, searching for some explanation, some thread of logic she might have missed. The memory of two particularly vicious individuals, their eyes glowing an unnatural crimson, flashed through her mind.

"The curse is because of her!" they had screamed, their once-human teeth as sharp as fangs.

Kora had tried to reason with them, to explain that her magic was for healing and defence, not curses or mutations. But they wouldn't listen. The rocks they'd hurled at her had struck with inhuman strength, knocking her to the ground.

The scene replayed in vivid detail: the gathering crowd, the raised pitchforks glinting in the stormy light, the growing panic as more residents of Northfox succumbed to the mysterious affliction. Kora remembered the horror she'd felt when two of the cursed population had suddenly bolted into the forest, beyond her reach before she could even attempt to help them.

"I only wanted to help," she whispered, the words lost in the howling wind.

She recalled the terror of fleeing through the wheat field, the townsfolk in pursuit. It struck her now as odd how they'd never quite managed to catch her. Had there been hesitation in their actions? A flicker of doubt in their eyes? Or was that just wishful thinking on her part?

Exhaustion began to seep into Kora's bones, momentarily dampening the fire of her anger. She needed shelter, a place to rest and gather her thoughts.

She made her way through the forest, following a series of distinct marks she had deliberately carved into the trees. Each one served as a signpost, guiding her towards a hidden sanctuary she had prepared long ago; she had never imagined she would need it under such dire circumstances.

Upon her arrival to the familiar spot, the mouth of the cave yawned before her, a welcome respite from the relentless storm. The moment she stepped inside, Kora immediately noticed the cool, dry air and the walls softly glowing with bioluminescent minerals. She moved further into the sheltered area and sank onto a pile of furs, her body finally giving in to the exhaustion she'd been fighting.

As she lay there, staring at the stalactites overhead, she thought about how they resembled the teeth of the cursed. She frowned, recalling the auras she'd observed from the afflicted. There had been something off, something... foreign.

"Could it have been that stranger?" she murmured.

Her eyes grew heavy, the question lingering unanswered as she drifted into an uneasy slumber, the storm still raging beyond her sanctuary.

***

As the last echoes of the townsfolk's anger faded into the storm-wracked night, a stranger emerged from the shadows at the edge of the crowd. A formidable figure, he stood tall, his presence a palpable weight in the air. In one gnarled hand, he clutched a smooth wooden staff, its top curving slightly as if reaching for the tumultuous sky. With his free hand, he absentmindedly twirled his long grey beard, a smile spreading across his weathered face like a crack in ancient stone.

His deep blue eyes, sharp as shards of ice, flashed with satisfaction as he watched the townsfolk disperse. Their earlier bravado had melted away, leaving behind a miasma of unease and whispered doubts.

"Was chasing Kora away the right thing to do?" a portly man with a worried expression murmured, his voice barely audible above the howling wind. "She's been so helpful to us..."

"What choice did we have?" his companion responded, casting a fearful glance over his shoulder. "By the time we realised the wizard was lying about Kora being responsible for the curse, we..."

A derisive snort cut through their hushed conversation. The old stranger approached, his robes inexplicably dry despite the deluge that had soaked everyone else.

"You had no choice," he confirmed invasively, his voice rough as gravel as he loomed over the cowering men, a cruel smirk curling his lips. "I advise you not to debate this any further – unless you want to end up like your friends who ran off into the forest."

The wizard's shadow seemed to grow, stretching unnaturally in the darkness until it engulfed the two men. They bowed their heads, murmuring apologies and agreements, their fear unmistakable. Pleased with their response, the wizard waved a dismissive hand and left them to worry.

As he moved through the town, the crowds parted before him like a dark sea. His every step left behind a footprint of swirling black and blue – puddles of loose mana that seemed to hunger for the very essence of life around them. Even the least magically inclined townsfolk instinctively recoiled from these ethereal pools.

Fate, however, was not kind to all. An orc, in his haste to reach the safety of his home, accidentally stumbled into one of the puddles, the effect immediate and horrifying. His grey flesh paled as if all vitality was being leeched away. Veins bulged unnaturally beneath his skin as he let out a strangled gasp. As he clutched at the suddenly prominent tusks jutting from his lower jaw, tears streamed from his small eyes. He limped towards his house, his strength entirely sapped. He would be useless in the fields tomorrow. How would he provide for his family now?

A human woman nearby shook her head, her hand flying to her mouth in shock.

"Not Olaf," she whispered, her voice thick with despair. "He didn't deserve that. If this stranger is capable of doing that so effortlessly, I fear what he could do next."

Standing beside the woman, an elderly elf nodded grimly in agreement before gently leading her away from the nightmarish scene. As they retreated, the shadows nearby seemed to gather strength, swallowing what little light remained. It was as if darkness itself bent to the wizard's will.

In a nearby alley, a goblin whispered to his companion, his sharp teeth glinting in the fading light.

"Normally the shadows are our sanctuary – a place of comfort. The wizard is turning them against us all."

His friend, a fellow goblin with bat-like ears twitching nervously, nodded in agreement. His lime-green skin gleamed slightly as he ran his tongue over his prominent fangs.

"Indeed," he grumbled. "Did you see the teeth on the cursed? They looked sharper than ours. That's a bad omen."

As whispers of fear and doubt spread through the town like a contagion, the wizard continued his slow, deliberate walk. Though his expression remained neutral, it was evident that inwardly, he relished the horrified reactions of those around him. With the only potential challenger out of the picture, there was no one left to oppose him. He was free to indulge his every whim and desire.

He approached a simple wooden house, its tan roof holding strong against the relentless storm. He entered without ceremony, stretching as the door closed behind him. He then collapsed into a sturdy rocking chair, chuckling to himself at the thought of the poor soul who no longer lived here.

After a few moments of quiet concentration, he tapped his staff gently against the wooden floor. Dark green mist began to rise from the ground, swirling and seeping into the staff as if drawn by an invisible force. The wizard held firm to the magical item as it absorbed energy, slowly draining the vitality from the entire town.

Outside, the effects were subtle but unmistakable. Grass withered at an accelerated rate. Animals became gaunt. None of the townsfolk dared to speak out, fearing they might end up like their cursed friends in the forest.

As the night deepened, a husband and wife stood at the edge of a chicken coop, their faces etched with worry. The husband bent down to inspect a bird lying on its side. It was weak and emaciated, despite having been healthy before.

"This hen won't last much longer, and neither will any of us if we can't do anything to stave off our hunger," he whispered. "Chasing Kora away was a huge mistake."

"I agree," his wife said solemnly, her voice heavy with regret. "But what could we have done? We'll just have to comply with the wizard and hope he doesn't destroy the entire town in the process. I don't want to end up like those poor souls in the forest."

***

Deep in the forest, far from the fearful whispers of the town, red eyes gleamed in the darkness. The air was thick with the scent of decay and damp earth, an unpleasant blend that clung to every leaf and branch. A deer's agonised scream pierced the night, only to be cut short as the innocent being was ripped apart. Blood splattered on the ground, illuminated for a brief moment by a flash of lightning, which tore across the sky to reveal twisted figures hunched over their prey.

Gnashing jaws tore into flesh, the cursed townsfolk finally finding the nourishment they craved. Bones cracked under powerful jaws as marrow was sucked greedily from splintered femurs. Claws that were once gentle human hands now raked through sinew and muscle, desperate to consume every morsel of their unfortunate victim. As the cursed feasted, their monstrous forms silhouetted against the stormy night, a primal hunger was sated. But with it came the chilling realisation that they could never return to their former lives.

The storm raged on, raindrops mingling with tears from eyes still holding a flicker of humanity. Lightning illuminated faces contorted in a grotesque mixture of ecstasy and horror – ecstasy at the fulfilment of their insatiable hunger, horror at what they had become. They were lost to the curse now, forever changed by the wizard's cruel magic.

One of the creatures let out a sorrowful howl, mourning the loss of their previous form. Nearby, others groaned in empathy. As the last scraps of venison disappeared down rabid throats, they all raised their heads to the cloud-covered moon, releasing a collective howl that echoed both triumph and despair.

They carried with them the weight of their actions and the knowledge that this night of terror would be the first of many. The curse had taken hold, and in its grip, they would remain – caught between two worlds, belonging to neither.

***

Back in the town, as the bloody feast continued in the forest, the wizard smiled to himself. His plan was unfolding perfectly. With Kora gone and the residents of Northfox cowed into submission, nothing stood in the way of his ultimate goal. As he drifted off to sleep, lulled by the sound of the storm and the steady drain of life force into his staff, he dreamed of the power that would soon be his to command.

Chapter Two

The relentless rain had turned the once-lush field into a muddy quagmire. Kora, her lithe elven form drenched and shivering, was on her hands and knees, frantically searching for a necklace she had only recently realised was missing. The necklace wasn't sentimentally valuable or special, but she figured that, having been chased from her home, she might need something of worth to trade for food and shelter. She cursed under her breath, berating herself for having dropped it.

As her fingers sifted through the sodden earth, Kora allowed herself a moment of bleak reflection. How quickly her life had unravelled, thrusting her into this nightmarish scenario.

Her search was abruptly interrupted by a deafening crack of thunder. The sound reverberated through her body, causing her to lose balance and fall face-first into the mud. As she scrambled to right herself, a shriek of surprise escaped her lips when a blinding flash of white light split the sky. Lightning struck the ground just metres away, the proximity sending shudders of panic coursing through her tense muscles.

The storm's fury seemed to intensify, focusing its wrath on this small patch of field. Above Kora, the clouds began to swirl in a circular formation, reminiscent of a miniature hurricane's eye. Her heart pounded frantically as more lightning bolts rained down around her, creating a dazzling, terrifying spectacle. Yet, miraculously, not a single bolt touched her.

Kneeling vulnerable and afraid, Kora was surrounded by a constant barrage of lightning that illuminated everything in sight. Strangely, the harsh light didn't harm her eyes, nor did the thunderous crashes assault her ears. Instead, she became aware of an otherworldly melody – the lightning itself seemed to be singing a haunting tune that filled the air around her.

Slowly, Kora's terror gave way to a cautious curiosity. She reached up, brushing aside strands of hair that clung to her face, the rainwater making their usual chestnut colour appear darker. Her azure eyes, wide with wonder, scanned the peculiar scene before her. A massive shadow began to form within the swirling clouds above, its shape gradually becoming more distinct.

With a thunderous impact that shook the earth, a colossal beast descended into the circular lightning field. Kora's breath caught in her throat as she beheld the magnificent creature – a dragon, its crimson scales gleaming in the light. Perched atop the dragon was a figure who demanded equal attention: an elderly man with slicked-back white hair and light stubble on his chin. His pale, scarred skin contrasted vividly with the flowing light-grey robes he wore.

Kora's gaze was drawn to the man's eyes – glowing amber irises that matched the aura surrounding him. In his somewhat wrinkled hand, he held a smooth mahogany wand, which he rested casually on the dragon's shoulder.

Unable to contain her curiosity, Kora inspected the dragon more closely. Its large build was overlapped with red scales that glinted like polished garnet. A sharp dorsal fin ran down its back, which the rider carefully avoided. Its sides were flanked with bat-like wings, each membrane taut and veined, hinting at the power they held. Its neck arched gracefully, reminiscent of a swan's, yet covered in thick, protective scales. The head, however, was unmistakably reptilian, with a crocodilian shape that gave it an air of ancient menace. This was a powerful, exceptional dragon, certainly not one native to these parts. Its presence was as foreign as it was awe-inspiring, a reminder of the distant lands and unknown realms it presumably hailed from.

Finally, Kora's attention returned to the mysterious rider.

"Who are you?" she asked, her tone a blend of fascination and wariness.

Without a word, the man began to rise from the dragon's back, floating effortlessly into the air. Kora blinked in disbelief as he performed a series of graceful flips and twirls.

It was as if gravity held no sway over him. After this impressive aerial display, he descended, landing before her with a flourish.

"Sir Wizard Bargot, at your service, lady elf," he announced with theatrical flair. "I see you have come into a predicament. I would very much like to mend that."

Kora opened her mouth to enquire further, but Wizard Bargot spoke first.

"Hold still!" he declared with a booming voice.

The shock of the command caused Kora to cry out, her body tensing instinctively. A flicker of anger ignited in her eyes, and she felt the stirrings of a minor spell forming in her mind. A small, humbling jolt wouldn't hurt him, she thought.

Before she could act on this impulse, Wizard Bargot thrust his hand forward, delivering a light but unexpected tap to Kora's forehead. The sudden contact made her lose her balance, causing her to rock back on her heels and nearly topple over from her kneeling position.

"Ow!" she said, more startled and annoyed than hurt. "What are you…"

The wizard held up a single finger, signalling for Kora to wait. Emerald lights began to materialise in the air, tracing the outlines of a bow and quiver of arrows.

"What's going on?" Kora whispered, her frustration giving way to amazement.

"We have much to discuss," Wizard Bargot began, his tone suddenly businesslike. "You have an evil fellow to deal with back in Northfox. He's sapping its power, turning its residents into monsters. I trust that you will want to do something about that. Take this bow and quiver of arrows that I've conjured. They will help you on your quest."

Kora, still soaked to the bone and struggling to process this turn of events, placed a hand on her forehead. Never before had she experienced such a bizarre interaction.

"I don't understand," she said, her voice tinged with suspicion. "Wizards don't randomly help people. From all of my studies, they especially hate elves due to our powerful arcane abilities, which typically clash with their chaotic nature. Why would you help me?"

Wizard Bargot scratched his head thoughtfully before nodding, as if having come to a decision. In a snap of inspiration, he raised his wand, tapping an invisible point in the air. After a brief pause that left Kora even more on edge, lights began to form in the shape of a violin and bow.

Pocketing his wand, the wizard reached for the ethereal instrument.

"Allow me to show you," he said with a grandiose gesture.

As he began to play the magical violin, his expert movements coaxing a haunting melody, soundless lightning struck the ground between them. Kora found herself transfixed as the light formed into two distinct figures – one resembling Wizard Bargot, and the other resembling an older, more withered man.

The vision unfolded like a silent, luminous play. The Wizard Bargot figure raised his arms, sending bolts of lightning towards the older man – seemingly an evil wizard who countered with dark, corrupted tendrils of light. Their battle raged across the sky, neither gaining the upper hand. As the wizards clashed, the lights formed swiftly moving clouds and a sun that rose and set rapidly, compressing the passage of time into mere moments where days became months, and months became years.

The magical duel persisted, and just as it seemed the stalemate would never end, the tide turned – but not in Wizard Bargot's favour. Forced to flee, he watched helplessly as cracks of corrupted light began to spread across the land.

As the final notes of the violin faded, so too did the vision. When Wizard Bargot bowed, the instrument vanished from his hands.

"You see," he explained, his voice sombre, "Northfox has been cursed by Wizard Wygor, the man you saw in the vision. I hate him more than I hate elves. I can't defeat him, but I'm confident that an elf can. Kora, I have been aware of you for some time now; you would be perfect for this. Agree to defeat

Wizard Wygor, and the bow and arrows are yours."

Kora's eyes narrowed, her posture straightening as she rolled her shoulders back.

"How can I trust you?" she said, making no effort to hide her cynicism.

"You can't," Wizard Bargot replied frankly, doing little to offer reassurance, "but look at you: you've got nothing. What have you got to lose?"

Kora knew she shouldn't trust wizards. Her upbringing had taught her to be wary of their tricks and deceptions. But the circumstances were dire. She had been chased from her town, no longer had her bow and arrows, and was now exceptionally vulnerable. Her instincts screamed caution, but the reality of her situation couldn't be denied. She had so little to lose and desperately needed a weapon to defend herself. Besides, she thought, the town had once been her home, and the people her friends. If she could defeat Wizard Wygor and break the curse, it would prove to everyone, once and for all, that she wasn't behind the chaos she stood accused of.

As she looked into Wizard Bargot's eyes, searching for any sign of deceit, Kora thought about her options. She could refuse and continue wandering defenceless, or she could take a chance and accept his offer. The risk of trusting a wizard was great, but the need for a weapon – and the need to prove herself to the townsfolk – was greater.

"Ok," she said, resignation in her tone. "I don't fully understand wizard feuds, and I'd rather not do anyone else's bidding, but you clearly know what I'm up against, and so yes, I accept your offer."

"And so you should," Wizard Bargot replied delightedly as he offered Kora her new weaponry. "I promise you, Kora, you won't regret this. The bow and arrows I'm gifting to you are like no weapon you have ever used before; they will always meet the intended mark of their owner."

Still afraid that she hadn't made the best decision, Kora accepted the bow and quiver of arrows.

"You will need to train hard, young elf," Wizard Bargot cautioned as he remounted his dragon. "Wizard Wygor has many tricks up his sleeve. Hone your magical and tactical skills, then go and meet him in combat. Despite the power of your superior weaponry, the prospect of victory cannot be taken for granted."

With those parting words, Wizard Bargot and his dragon took to the skies, disappearing into the clouds. As they vanished from sight, the supernatural storm began to dissipate, leaving behind only a heavy rain.

Alone in the field once more, a sense of purpose slowly replaced Kora's earlier confusion and fear. She couldn't shake the feeling of being a pawn in a larger game, but she yearned to see Northfox restored to its former state, even if that meant taking down one wizard for the benefit of another.

As she contemplated her next move, Kora couldn't help but marvel at the mysterious and often self-serving nature of wizards. At least Wizard Bargot had given her a chance to save the town and reclaim her place there.

Still, she mused wryly, some directions to the nearest village would have been helpful. After being out in the rain for so long, she was eager to find a tavern where she could settle down comfortably for a while.

Chapter Three

With the dawn of a new day, the rain had thinned to a gradual stop, but the heavy clouds lingering overhead threatened more to come. Kora stood in a clearing, shivering slightly as an autumn chill swept through the area. Winter's icy fingers weren't far behind, she knew, and being chased from her warm home couldn't have come at a worse time.

As she turned to retreat to the cave and gather her thoughts, a loud rustling noise froze her in place. She whirled around, her hand instinctively reaching for her new bow.

When Kora's eyes locked onto the figure ambling through the wet grass, she soon realised it was a young woman, barely out of her teens. Her curly brown hair was matted by the rain, her pale skin glistened with moisture, and her brown eyes were wide with a mixture of relief and exhaustion. As recognition dawned, Kora's posture stiffened, her arms crossing defensively over her chest.

"I've found you!" the young woman exclaimed, her rounded ears marking her as human.

Kora's eyes narrowed as she scrutinised the approaching woman. Her hands were visible and empty, suggesting no immediate threat. Though wary, Kora couldn't detect any malice in the woman's steady gaze or the calm, almost curious, tilt of her head. Trusting her instincts, Kora allowed herself to relax slightly.

"Hey," Kora said softly. "Are you alright?"

The human woman nodded enthusiastically, her face beaming with a smile and her eyes sparkling with unmistakable admiration.

"I'm Sophie," said the woman, still catching her breath, "from Northfox. The way they treated you wasn't right. I've looked up to you ever since you saved my family from that chimera. The way you used your bow and arrow to protect us was astounding."

The memory helped to put Kora at ease.

"Hi there, Sophie," she said, offering a weary smile. "I'm honoured to hear that, but you ran all this way to tell me? Won't the townsfolk be angry at you for fraternising with their supposed enemy?"

"Perhaps," Sophie said with surprising confidence as she straightened, pushing a damp curl from her face. "That's why I won't be going back. I want to help you, Kora. I watched what happened from the shadows, but I couldn't catch everything. Northfox is in a terrible state. People are dying. In the hysteria of it all, terrible decisions are being made – like the one they came up with to chase you out! You've helped us so much over the years with healing and defence. It's time I returned the favour."

Kora blinked, caught off guard by the earnest offer. A lone tear traced its way down her cheek, which she hastily wiped away. The weight of her isolation lifted ever so slightly. She wasn't alone in this anymore.

"That's... that's much appreciated," Kora managed, her voice thick with emotion. "I need all the help I can get. I have been informed that Northfox has in fact been taken over by a wizard: Wizard Wygor. You see this bow and arrows I've got here? They were given to me by Wizard Bargot; he has entrusted me with a mission to defeat Wizard Wygor."

"Wizard Wygor!" Sophie said angrily. "So that's his name! I wish him nothing but the worst. I saw my parents wither away because of his magic."

Sophie's lip quivered, her expression one of sadness and shame. Kora felt a pang of sympathy for the young woman. Shaking her head, she reached out and placed a comforting hand on her shoulder.

"I'm so sorry, Sophie," she murmured, her voice tinged with sorrow. "No one should have to endure such pain. I understand your anger, your wish for justice. You're holding strong, not letting despair consume you. That counts for a lot. Come on, let's get to a safe area and start planning our next move."

The unlikely pair made their way through the clearing and into the forest beyond. As the storm clouds began to part, the wildlife came alive around them. The birds burst into cheerful song, while colourful squirrels engaged in comical chases with mischievous, fuzzy two-legged creatures – gremlins with bat-like ears who often succeeded in their nut-thieving escapades. Kora found herself smiling at nature's resilience, a reminder that pockets of peace still existed in this troubled world.

Sophie walked a few paces behind, her shoulders slumped under the weight of recent tragedies. Though she tried to keep her tone upbeat when speaking, waves of despair radiated from her. Kora sensed it, but chose not to press, allowing the young woman space to process her emotions.

When they arrived at the mouth of the cave she was familiar with, Kora set about gathering firewood. She arranged the wet logs into a neat pile, then began a low chant. Steam rose from the wood as her spell dried it to desert-like perfection. However, when she tried to ignite the fire with a snap of her fingers, nothing happened. Frowning, she tried again, only to be met with the same result.

"I could have sworn the logs were completely dry," she muttered, touching the wood to confirm. "I hope after everything that's happened, I'm not losing my touch!"

"Allow me," Sophie offered, shuffling forward with a soft smile.

She whispered a few words, and after a brief pause, flames sprang to life among the logs. Kora blinked in surprise, regarding the human with newfound curiosity.

Sophie reached into her worn leather bag and carefully withdrew a cloth-wrapped parcel, from which the subtle scent of dried fruits escaped. It was a modest offering, indicative of a meal packed hurriedly under pressing circumstances.

"It takes humans a while to learn magic when they don't resort to darker methods," Kora mused aloud, her mind whirling with questions. "You look to be in your early twenties, just a few years younger than me. How long have you been practicing?"

"Just about over a decade," Sophie admitted, a modest blush rising in her cheeks. "You rescued my family when I was nine. You were just a teenager then! It left quite an impression. I wanted to work hard and be like you. Of course, I'm nowhere near as good as you – you're far more advanced. I'm pleased that I can light a fire, but a simple spell like that wouldn't be useful in combat."

"Don't underestimate yourself," Kora said. "It's worth bearing in mind that whilst elves are born with innate magical abilities, they often hit a plateau earlier than humans with a desire to learn. Most elves don't bother to push themselves, relying on their natural gifts. Even though I've invested a lot of time and work into my own magic, I still rely on my bow and arrows more than magic in a fight."

As they shared the dried fruits around the comforting warmth of the fire, their conversation drifted to lighter topics, carefully avoiding mention of Sophie's parents.

"I confess," Kora said eventually, "I don't know where to go next."

Sophie's eyes lit up. She rummaged through her bag to produce a map.

"I always try to plan ahead," she said with a grin. "I have many tools to help us. This map shows key points for villages that specialise in magical training. I've travelled quite a bit, seeking knowledge wherever I can find it."

Kora gasped, accepting the map with reverence. Her finger traced the inked paths and markings, a world of possibilities opening before her. She handed it back to Sophie with a grateful nod.

"I already don't know what I'd do without you," Kora admitted. "The first path looks to be a long one. We might run into trouble. I don't mind, but..."

"More trouble means more training," Sophie said, her optimism shining through. "I'm not the best in combat though. I prefer healing and navigation. Will that be alright?"

"Of course," said Kora, smiling at Sophie's endearing approach. "Healing skills are just as vital as combat skills. Sure, I have some healing magic, but I doubt it's as powerful as yours, especially if that's been your focus for all these years."

As night fell, the distant howls, roars, and screeches of nocturnal predators filled the air. The rustling of trees signalled the approach of owl-bears – creatures best avoided by both elves and humans alike. With caution, Kora and Sophie retreated into the cave, seeking refuge from the dangers lurking beyond.

Inside the cave's cool embrace, Kora took charge, making sure Sophie had a comfortable sleeping area away from the cold draft and damp ground. They gathered dried leaves to cushion their makeshift beds, arranging them carefully beneath the furs to maximise comfort against the harsh terrain.

Pretending to be asleep to give Sophie some space, Kora observed silently as the young woman allowed herself a quiet cry, the echoes of her pent-up grief resonating in the stillness of the cave.

As Sophie eventually drifted off, Kora's mind raced. She tossed and turned on her makeshift bed, the flickering light of the diminishing fire casting dancing shadows on the cave walls.

Just as the fire was about to burn out, Kora sat up suddenly, her gaze fixed on a large, fur-covered creature lumbering into the clearing. Its bear-like body had bloodstained claws, and its head was unmistakably that of an owl – an owl-bear.

The creature peered into the cave. As it moved to investigate further, the top of its feathered head struck an invisible barrier. After a moment of confused snuffling, the beast decided the effort wasn't worth it, and stomped off in search of easier prey.

Kora turned around to see Sophie sitting up, watching the owl-bear's retreat with a satisfied smirk on her lips.

"Ward enchantments strike again," Sophie murmured with amusement as she settled back down to sleep, her breaths soon becoming deep and even.

Kora couldn't help but be impressed. The human woman's ability to anticipate danger – and protect them from it – demonstrated a level of skill and maturity that could prove invaluable.

As the night wore on, Kora's sleep was restless, haunted by dreams of battling the evil wizard and the dark curse he had inflicted upon the innocent. Despite the turmoil, however, a glimmer of optimism shone through. With Sophie by her side as a formidable ally, Kora dared to hope that maybe – just maybe – they would have a fighting chance against their enemy.

Chapter Four

Kora awoke with a start, her eyes fluttering open as the first rays of dawn filtered into the cave. She stretched languidly, working out the kinks in her muscles from a night spent on the hard ground. As she sat up, her keen elven senses picked up the telltale crackle of a fire outside – a sure sign that Sophie was already up.

Running her fingers through her tangled hair, Kora winced as she worked out the knots. Once she felt presentable, she emerged from the cave's cool darkness into the crisp morning air. Sophie sat perched on a moss-covered boulder, tending to the small fire. When she looked up, she offered Kora a wan smile that didn't quite reach her eyes.

"Breakfast is ready," she announced, gesturing to the spit of roasting meat above the flames. "I've already been hunting. I didn't sleep well. The furs were comfortable enough, but my dreams... The past haunts me, and the future feels so uncertain."

Kora nodded in silent understanding. She too had battled her own demons in the night. Pushing those thoughts aside, she settled next to the fire, savouring the familiar scent of spices wafting from the meat. It was a bittersweet reminder of home, but she forced herself to focus on the present. Today was about moving forward.

As they ate, dew glistened on vibrant leaves, and a heavy mist clung to the ground, sending a chill through both women. Despite the warmth radiating from the fire, the surrounding coldness still seeped in, causing Kora to shiver. She briefly retreated to the cave to retrieve extra furs. Draping one over her shoulders, she offered the other to Sophie, satisfied that they would ensure maximum protection for the journey ahead.

After dismantling any signs of their stay at the cave, they set off. Sophie walked a few paces behind Kora, consulting her map and offering quiet directions. All around them, the forest teemed with life: wary deer observed them from behind thick tree trunks, while a mischievous winged monkey chittered overhead, eyeing the two women with clear interest.

As they walked, a symphony of birdsong filled the air. Tiny, jewel-toned feathered creatures flitted from branch to branch, their melodies uninterrupted by the two travellers below. The rich scent of loamy earth mingled with the sharp tang of evergreens, creating an intoxicating perfume that spoke of wilderness and adventure.

By midday, the dense forest gave way to a well-worn dirt path, its surface rutted by countless wagon wheels and horse hooves. Kora and Sophie's spirits lifted at this sign of civilisation, their pace quickening with renewed energy.

"You're going to love the village," Sophie enthused, a genuine smile lighting up her face. "It's... different there. They judge you on who you are, not what you are. In a world so quick to label things as evil, it's a breath of fresh air. Prejudice has no place there."

"That sounds good," said Kora, her eyes sparkling with excitement. "I hope they will make us feel welcome."

"I'm confident they will," said Sophie.

"Wait... do you see that?" Kora exclaimed, her gaze suddenly focusing on something in the distance.

Three small figures gradually came into view, their moss-green skin standing out against the earthy tones of the path. They wore ill-fitting chainmail over rough wool clothing, and as they drew closer, Kora could make out their bat-like ears and unnervingly sharp teeth.

"Goblins," she murmured, tension creeping into her voice. "I've heard they sometimes work for unsavoury types, but let's not jump to conclusions."

Despite her words, Kora's hand instinctively moved closer to her bow.

The situation grew more ominous as Kora spotted the bristling onyx-furred wolf trudging behind the goblins. It was muzzled, tethered to a small wagon overflowing with plants that seemed to radiate a malevolent aura. Every instinct screamed danger, but Kora was determined to avoid conflict if possible.

"Greetings, friends," she called out cautiously as they approached.

Sophie remained silent, her watchful gaze never leaving the goblin trio.

The goblins studied the two women intently, wicked grins spreading across their faces. They muttered amongst themselves in a guttural language before the apparent leader stepped forward. Golden hoops dangled from his pointed ears, and a web of scars crisscrossed his leathery skin.

"Well, well," the goblin said, a low growl in his voice, his gnarled hand hovering over the knife on his belt. "You folks must be from Northfox. Long way from home, ain'tcha? Merchants maybe? Don't see no cart with ya."

"We're just passing through," Kora replied, her voice firm as steel.

"Right. Passing through," said the goblin, his tone dripping with sarcasm as his eyes narrowed with suspicion. "Well, unfortunately for you, ya shouldn't have left town."

In a blur of motion, the goblin unsheathed his knife. It flashed with an eerie green glow. Kora barely had time to react before searing pain exploded in her arm. She stumbled backwards, blood flowing freely from the wound. Seething with anger, she lashed out, her other hand forming into a fist and connecting solidly with the goblin's face, sending him sprawling.

Chaos erupted. The other two goblins nocked arrows, their bows drawn and ready to fire. Kora back-pedalled frantically, her mind racing to formulate a plan. Behind her, she heard Sophie's urgent whispers as healing magic knitted the worst of her wound closed.

Pushing through the distraction of the surreal sensation in her skin, Kora reached for her bow. The weapon seemed to hum with energy as she drew it, its emerald glow stark even in the daylight. Time seemed to slow as she nocked an arrow, her elven reflexes giving her a precious advantage.

The lead goblin charged, but Kora's arrow found its mark, burying itself deep in the creature's chest. He crumpled to the ground, lifeless before he hit the dirt.

Two arrows whistled past, missing Kora by mere inches. A third found its target, sinking into her shoulder with a sickening thud. Pain bloomed around the entire area, but she gritted her teeth, forcing herself to focus.

Another arrow flew from her bow, striking the neck of one of the two remaining goblins. It wasn't a killing blow, but crimson blood dribbled from the wound, causing his next shot to miss.

Suddenly, Kora felt a strange sensation in her shoulder. The arrow seemed to push itself out of her flesh, clattering to the ground as the wound sealed shut. Sophie's healing magic coursed through her, renewing her strength.

Emboldened, Kora nocked another arrow. As she released it, time seemed to slow. The arrow streaked through the air, trailing viridian light. It struck the second archer squarely in the chest, rendering him lifeless with almost immediate effect.

The final goblin, clutching his bleeding neck, stumbled and fell. His eyes were wide with fear as Kora approached, another arrow nocked and ready. With a blend of compassion and grim certainty, she took careful aim. The arrow found its mark, piercing the goblin's temple and ending his suffering instantly.

As the dust settled, Kora surveyed the scene. Three dead goblins, their blood staining the earth. The mysterious cart sat abandoned, its cargo giving off an aura of wrongness that made her skin crawl. And then there was the wolf, its muzzled snout quivering with barely-contained rage.

Kora approached Sophie, who looked shaken but unharmed.

"Are you alright?" Kora asked, her voice laced with concern.

Sophie nodded, already moving to examine Kora's wounds.

"Hold still," Sophie instructed, her hands glowing with verdant healing energy. "This will help."

Kora winced as Sophie's shimmering hands gently pressed against her wounds. The healing magic flowed through her, warming her skin. She marvelled at Sophie's skill.

As the pain subsided, Kora's attention returned to the wolf. Its fury seemed to be at breaking point, and to her utter astonishment, it spoke.

"What are you waiting for?" he said with a snarl, his voice rough and guttural. "Get this thing off me! Those morons had the audacity to keep me bound like this. If you're not going to eat the bodies, then I will!"

Kora blinked in disbelief. A talking wolf? She knew she needed to be cautious.

"How do I know you won't attack us?" she asked the wolf.

The wolf snorted, a sound that lingered between amusement and irritation.

"Fair question," he answered. "I've been in servitude to those vermin for years. By freeing me, you've earned my debt. Why would I bite the hand that feeds me – or more accurately, the hand that doesn't hold me against my will? The name's Deerbane. Bane for short."

Kora and Sophie exchanged uncertain glances.

"Is this a good idea?" Kora whispered, leaning in closely to consult with Sophie.

"He seems... well, not exactly nice, but at least not openly hostile," Sophie said with a shrug of her shoulders. "We could give him the benefit of the doubt."

Kora approached Bane cautiously, her steps deliberate and measured. She reached out slowly, her fingers brushing against the rough texture of the muzzle as he watched her with wary amber eyes. With steady hands, she carefully unclasped the fastenings and removed the restraint, revealing the wolf's powerful jaws beneath.

Next, she moved to the ropes on his legs, taking care to free each limb methodically. Bane remained surprisingly still, co-operating entirely.

As the last knot came undone, the wolf stretched his limbs, testing his newfound freedom. Kora stood back, watching with both relief and curiosity.

True to his word, Bane lunged for the nearest goblin corpse, tearing into the flesh with savage efficiency. Kora grimaced, but didn't intervene. She'd seen enough of nature's brutality to know this was simply the way of things.

"We'll need to be extra vigilant on the road now," Kora said to Sophie. "I hate to think what might have happened without your healing skills."

"You're more than welcome," Sophie said with a warm smile. "That's what friends are for. We all need backup in combat."

For a brief moment, Kora allowed herself to savour the feeling of camaraderie that Sophie's words had brought. She was promptly interrupted as Bane approached, his face stained with goblin blood.

"Before either of you ladies panic," he said, "I'm not about to attack. I have no interest in doing so. I am curious: What brings you to these dangerous roads? It's no place for small parties, even if you both seem capable."

"We're on a quest to defeat an evil wizard in Northfox," Kora explained, sensing no reason for deception. "But first, we're on our way to…"

She glanced at Sophie, suddenly blanking on the name.

"Whimsville," Sophie answered, double-checking her map to be certain.

Bane sat back on his haunches, considering this information.

"A noble quest," he said approvingly. "I find myself without purpose or pack. You two seem pleasant enough. Perhaps I could join you?"

Kora hesitated, studying the wolf.

"Hmm…" she mused. "Are you a human who has been cursed to be a wolf? Or are you a natural-born wolf with the exceptional ability to communicate?"

"The latter," Bane replied. "My pack is long dead. I wandered alone until I saved a powerful elf who blessed me with speech and heightened intelligence. I've been searching for a new purpose ever since. My time with those goblins who captured me was an unfortunate episode along the way."

"Those three were awful," Sophie chimed in. "The kind who give all goblins a bad name. Some are aggressive, true, but others are decent and work hard to provide valuable trade."

Kora nodded, impressed by Sophie's knowledge. She weighed their options carefully before responding to Bane.

"Alright, Bane," she said. "You can join us."

The wolf's tail wagged slightly as he turned back to finish his grisly feast. Meanwhile, Kora approached the abandoned wagon, her stomach churning at the sight of its cargo. Dark green vines bristled with wicked thorns, and jagged leaves bore ominous crimson and gold markings. A palpable aura of malice emanated from the plants.

"Bane," she called, "do you know what these are?"

"Yes," he said as he looked up, his snout wrinkling in disgust. "They reek of trouble. I've never witnessed them being put to use, but the goblins transported them often. They were headed for Northfox this time. After recent events there, that can only mean ill tidings."

"Sophie," said Kora, her expression hardening with concern, "can you burn these?"

"Of course," Sophie replied. "Stand back, everyone. They might be cursed."

As Kora and Bane retreated to a safe distance, Sophie called upon her magic. Small, controlled flames erupted from her hands, swirling and dancing with intense heat. The sinister plants caught fire instantly, crackling and burning with an eerie hiss. Kora watched with a mixture of awe and relief as the flames consumed the foreboding flora.

Despite the cart's potential usefulness for their journey, Kora knew it was better to let it burn alongside the sinister plants. The risk of touching them to clear the cart would have been far too high. Soon, only drifting ash and the lingering scent of smoke remained from the consumed wood.

"I'm going to take this," Sophie said as she bent to pick up the knife previously owned by the outspoken goblin. "I'll keep it safe in my bag."

With the immediate threat neutralised, the unlikely trio ventured onwards, the afternoon sun warm on their backs. Kora found herself feeling grateful for her new companions: for Sophie's wisdom and healing, and for Bane's raw strength and unique perspective. Perhaps together, they stood a chance against whatever darkness lay ahead.

Suddenly, a large shadow loomed over them. Kora immediately looked up, her keen eyes widening at the shocking sight above. A wyvern, its pearlescent scales glinting in the light, circled ominously overhead. Bane's fur bristled as he let out a low, rumbling growl.

"We must be in its hunting territory," Sophie observed anxiously, her voice tight with fear. "It probably sees us as a potential meal!"

Chapter Five

Kora nocked an arrow to her bow, the weaponry's verdant glow pulsing vibrantly. Shifting her weight, she planted one foot forward, assuming the perfect archer's stance.

The air crackled with tension as the wyvern's chest expanded, a telltale sign of the impending inferno. Scales along its neck began to glow an ominous orange, like embers stirring to life. The beast's eyes, yellow and slit-pupiled, fixed upon its prey with predatory focus. Then, in a terrifying instant, a ball of fire erupted from its maw, hurtling towards the group at devastating speed.

Kora braced herself, feeling the blistering heat as it approached. Just as the flames were about to engulf her, they slammed into an invisible barrier, the sudden impact sending ripples of energy cascading all around.

"I've got your back!" Sophie called out from behind.

Emboldened by her friend's protection, Kora drew back her bow. The enchanted arrow hummed with power as she took aim. The wyvern, undeterred, unleashed another torrent of fire. For a heart-stopping moment, Kora feared her shot would be incinerated. To her amazement though, the arrow pierced through the inferno unscathed, its magical properties proving their worth.

With unerring accuracy, the arrow found its mark, burying itself deep in the wyvern's chest. The beast's next fiery assault died in its throat, leaving it momentarily stunned.

Bane seized the opportunity, his form a blur of midnight fur and gleaming fangs. His eyes blazed with predatory hunger as he launched himself at the wyvern. As his powerful jaws clamped down on the creature's leg, tearing through scales and into tender flesh, blood sprayed in crimson arcs, painting his coat and the surrounding ground.

But the wyvern was far from defeated. With a vicious twist of its serpentine neck, it sank its teeth into Bane's shoulder.

Kora's mind raced, recognising the critical moment. In one fluid motion, she nocked two arrows simultaneously. Time seemed to slow as she released the bowstring, watching the projectiles whistle through the air. They struck true, embedding themselves beside her initial shot. The combined force shattered the wyvern's protective scales, piercing its heart.

With an ear-splitting shriek, the mighty beast swayed. Its eyes rolled back, and it toppled to the ground with an earth-shaking thud. Bane, still caught in the throes of battle lust, limped towards the fallen foe. Whilst his shoulder bled freely, he seemed oblivious to the pain, driven by an insatiable hunger.

Sophie approached the wyvern's carcass cautiously, her scholarly instincts taking over. She bent to examine its hide, her eyes lighting up with recognition.

"These scales are incredibly valuable," she said as she turned to retrieve the knife from her bag. "We can sell them when we reach the village – it'll help cover our expenses and then some."

As Sophie carefully harvested the scales, Kora retrieved her arrows. To her astonishment, they were completely unmarred – no splits, no scorching, not even a hint of blood. She marvelled at their craftsmanship, realising how crucial such durability would be for the challenges ahead.

Once Sophie had finished her work, she turned her attention to Bane. The wolf reluctantly paused his feast, allowing her healing magic to knit his wounds.

With everyone's injuries addressed, the trio resumed their journey.

The next two days proved arduous. They encountered another sinister group of goblins, dispatching them with greater efficiency. An aggressive owl-bear provided a moment of genuine fear, but working together as a strong team, the group prevailed. By the time Whimsville's outskirts came into view, exhaustion had settled deep into their bones.

The village itself was a revelation. Rustic buildings and horse-drawn wagons created a quaint backdrop, but it was the inhabitants that truly astonished Kora. Goblins strolled peacefully alongside humans. A well-groomed demon in merchant's garb engaged in friendly negotiations. Most surprising of all, a chimera – part lion, part goat, with a serpent for a tail – casually carried a bucket of water down the street.

As they made their way through the village, Sophie pointed out the imposing ogre guards. Standing as tall as the buildings themselves, their plates of armour gleamed in the fading sunlight. Despite their fearsome appearance, they exuded an air of calm vigilance.

Further down the road, a tavern beckoned to the travelling trio, its simplistic yet large sign – The Goblin's Keep – a beacon in the gathering dusk. The building itself was a sturdy, timber-framed structure, its walls weathered by time but exuding an undeniable charm. Ivy climbed up one side, its lush green tendrils weaving around the weathered wood, adding a vibrancy to the venerable façade.

With Sophie and Bane by her side, Kora entered through the heavy oak doors, which stood open and welcoming. She immediately noticed the atmosphere – warm and inviting compared to the emerging chill outside. A comforting heat emanated from a crackling fire that dominated one corner of the room. The firelight danced and flickered, casting playful shadows across the stone walls and wooden beams, giving the room an almost magical ambiance. The scent of roasting meat and freshly-baked bread mingled with the sweet aroma of spiced ale, creating an intoxicating blend that made Kora salivate, her stomach rumbling in anticipation.

Patrons filled the tavern, their faces flushed with laughter and good cheer as they gathered around tables crafted from rich, dark wood, polished to a shine by years of use. A friendly demon woman sat on a low stool near the hearth, her skin a deep crimson that glowed softly in the firelight. Her eyes, bright and mischievous, twinkled as her fingers expertly plucked the strings of a lute. The instrument seemed to come alive in her hands, producing enchanting melodies that floated through the air, creating an aura of tranquillity and joy.

Kora's eyes wandered to the bar at the far end of the room. Gathering her resolve, she headed towards it, her boots thudding softly against the well-worn wooden floor as Sophie and Bane followed behind.

Behind the bar, a goblin methodically polished glasses. He raised an eyebrow at Bane's presence.

"He's with us," Kora quickly explained.

The wolf settled beside her with deliberate nonchalance, punctuating the moment with an exaggerated yawn.

"You look like you're not from around here," the goblin said, curious rather than suspicious.

"You're right," said Kora. "I'm from Northfox. I was chased away by the townsfolk. They think I'm the one who cursed them."

"She didn't," Sophie chimed in. "I'm also from Northfox – a fact I'm not too proud of at the moment."

"A curse, eh?" said the goblin.

"Indeed," said Kora. "Wizard Wygor has taken over. We're exhausted from our travels, but once we've recuperated, we're going to head back to Northfox and put an end to his reign of tyranny."

A hush fell over the tavern. The goblin barkeeper set down his glass, his expression a blend of concern and grudging admiration.

"Wizard Wygor?" he said. "You do know how powerful he is, right?"

"We wouldn't dare underestimate him," Sophie said wisely.

"He's evil, that's for certain," the barkeeper said with conviction, his eyes darting between Kora, Sophie, and Bane, noting their obvious exhaustion. "You all look like you could use a drink and a good meal. On the house – just for tonight, mind you."

"Thank you," said Kora. "We appreciate it."

"No one's even considered taking on Wizard Wygor," the goblin explained as he poured generous measures of the tavern's finest ale. "But we've got folks who can train you – if you're up for weeks of blood, sweat, and tears."

"We would welcome that tremendously," said Kora.

"Yes," Sophie agreed. "What's happening in Northfox could just be the beginning. If we don't stop Wizard Wygor, nowhere will be safe."

"I like your gumption," the goblin barkeeper said with a chuckle, a wide grin spreading across his face. "The room is half-price for you three. But keep that under your hat – I've still got a business to run!"

He reached under the counter and pulled out a rolled-up map, spreading it out flat across the wooden surface. With a slender finger, he traced a path on it. Kora leaned in to observe, noting that the route led from the village to a secluded spot near a forest.

"There's a training ground not far from here," he said. "I'm sure they'd be eager to help you."

"Thank you," Kora said sincerely before turning to Sophie, who nodded in agreement.

"Follow me," the goblin barkeeper said, rolling up the map and passing it to Sophie, who tucked it away in her bag.

He led them through the bustling tavern and up a narrow staircase, the creaking wooden steps adding to the rustic charm of the place. At the end of a dimly lit hallway, he opened a door to a spacious guest room. It was simple but inviting, with two large beds covered in thick quilts. A small fireplace crackled in the corner, casting a warm glow. Noticing Bane, the goblin moved quickly, arranging a pile of blankets on the floor. He then nodded and left them to settle in.

Kora and Sophie each took a bed, while Bane curled up on the newly-arranged blankets. The fire's gentle heat and the room's snug atmosphere were a welcome relief after their arduous travels.

As Kora lay back, she felt the tension slowly leaving her body. Sophie was already drifting off, her breathing steady and calm. Bane closed his eyes and let out a contented sigh. Staring at the ceiling for a moment, Kora's mind raced with thoughts of the days to come, but for now, she allowed herself to embrace the softness of the bed.

Chapter Six

Dawn broke over Whimsville, painting the sky in hues of gold and pink. A gentle breeze carried fallen leaves down the cobblestone streets, their rustling a soft accompaniment to the village's awakening. Kora stepped out of the tavern into the crisp morning air, her long chestnut hair catching the sun's early rays like polished bronze. Sophie fell into step beside her, her curls neatly styled with the bone comb she'd brought from home.

"Where's Bane?" Sophie asked, glancing around for their wolfish companion.

"He'll meet us at the training grounds," Kora said, gesturing eastwards. "He says he doesn't fancy going to the shop with us."

As the two young women made their way down the dirt path, Whimsville came to life around them. In a nearby field, horses grazed lazily, their tails swishing at flies. A flock of chickens darted across their way, pursued by a border collie with a coat of flowing ebony and pearl. Kora paused, kneeling to offer her hand to the eager dog. It sniffed her fingers, gave a friendly bark, and then bounded off to resume its herding duties.

The shop's bell tinkled merrily as Kora and Sophie entered. Behind the counter stood a sight that gave even Kora pause – a troll, towering at eight feet tall, with skin the colour of deep emerald and tusks like polished ivory jutting from his lower jaw. Lime-green hair cascaded over the shoulders of an exquisitely tailored jacket. With black claws, he drummed a gentle rhythm on the countertop as his tufted tail swished back and forth.

"Welcome, guests!" the troll said in greeting, his voice surprisingly melodious. "Don't forget to check the sign for today's discounts. We've got some real bargains."

Kora approached the board, her azure eyes scanning the list. It included rope, canteens for carrying water, and dried meat – all at prices that seemed too good to be true.

"That's quite a deal," she remarked. "What's the occasion?"

"Trade's been hit hard," said the troll, his expression darkening slightly. "Although Whimsville itself has no wizard troubles, the black market always seems to thrive when there are problems elsewhere."

"So I've heard," Kora said solemnly as she gathered supplies. "As it happens, I'm here to stock up before facing one such wizard myself."

The troll's eyes widened, studying Kora with newfound respect.

"That's no small task," he said. "You look capable enough though. I'm glad my discounts have come at a good time for you."

Meanwhile, Sophie had drifted to a display of dried herbs. Their pungent aromas filled the air, mingling with the scent of old parchment and freshly cut wood that permeated the shop. Delicate glass jars filled with lotions sat nearby, their contents shimmering with promise. She carefully selected a few items, adding them to her woven basket.

As they approached the counter to pay, Sophie placed a reassuring hand on Kora's shoulder. With a wink, she produced two gleaming wyvern scales from her bag and placed them down in front of the troll.

The troll gasped, leaning in to examine the scales more closely.

"By the ancient woods!" he exclaimed in amazement. "Where did you come across these beauties? They'll cover your expenses, and then some!"

"You're welcome to them," Kora replied with a grin.

Smiling appreciatively, the troll reached beneath the counter and retrieved an ornate wooden box. Its red and gold paint gleamed in the shop's warm light. As he opened the lid, the rich aroma of coffee beans wafted out, so intoxicating it made Kora's mouth water.

"Take six," the troll offered. "Three each – on the house. They say these beans are enchanted – they'll keep you alert longer than ordinary coffee. They might come in handy for your quest."

Kora accepted the gift gratefully, sensing the potent magical aura surrounding the beans. As they bid farewell to the kind shopkeeper, she felt a renewed sense of purpose. The generosity of strangers, it seemed, could be found even in these troubled times.

Navigating away from the shop, Kora and Sophie made their way to the training grounds. Upon their arrival, they were met by the sight of a large field that stretched out before them. The vast expanse of lush, green grass was dotted with the occasional cluster of wildflowers, their colours vivid against the sea of green. Grazing goats, their coats speckled with patches of white and brown, meandered through the grass, serene and oblivious to the rigorous activity that typically filled the space.

Towering pines fringed the perimeter of the field, their branches swaying gently in the breeze. Bane lounged beneath one such tree, his jaws parted in a canine grin as he watched the goats with undisguised interest.

"I doubt those goats are on the menu, Bane," Kora called out.

She then tossed him a dried pig's ear from her newly acquired supplies. He caught it with ease and began to gnaw at it with eager bites.

"Give me half an hour with this, and I'll be ready for anything," he replied, prompting good-natured eye-rolls from both women.

As the sun climbed higher, Kora found herself face-to-face with her first combat instructor. Melvin, an orc whose presence exuded experience, cut an imposing figure. His grey skin was crisscrossed with old battle scars, and his muscles rippled beneath his sleeveless shirt. Short tusks jutted from his lower jaw, and his pointed ears were adorned with metallic piercings.

"Assume the wizard might set orcs on you as strong as me," Melvin said, a growl in his voice and his pig-like eyes glinting with determination. "You need to learn to face us head-on. Identify the lethal points, strike quickly, and be prepared to take a few hits yourself."

"That's fine by me," Kora replied graciously.

She reached for her bow and arrows, but as her fingers brushed the weapons, a realisation struck her: they were enchanted to always strike with brutal accuracy. Using them for practice wouldn't be beneficial, or indeed safe.

"Wait!" Kora called out, stopping Melvin just as he was about to continue. "My bow and arrows... they always hit their mark. I think I need regular weaponry for training."

"Good point," Melvin agreed. "You won't learn much if every shot's perfect... Hang on a moment."

Kora watched as Melvin strode over to a nearby rack of weapons, his movements fluid despite his bulky frame. He rummaged through the assortment of items before pulling out a plain, well-worn bow – with arrows to match. He then walked back to Kora and handed them to her with a nod.

"Here," he said. "They have seen a lot of use, but they'll do the job."

"Thanks," she said.

"Ok," he said loudly, his focus switching immediately as he moved to the opposite end of the training area. "Ready?"

"Ready," Kora confirmed, bracing herself for the challenge.

With a shockingly-loud roar, Melvin charged. His rubber axe whistled through the air, narrowly missing Kora's shoulder as she twisted away. Heart pounding, she fired an arrow, striking the orc's heavily-padded shoulder.

Kora's victory was short-lived. Melvin, with decades of experience, had anticipated her next move. As she darted sideways, he pivoted, bringing his axe around in a sweeping arc. The blunt weapon connected with her side, sending her flying. She landed hard on the ground, stars exploding behind her eyes.

Melvin approached, his battle fury giving way to concern. He extended a meaty hand, which Kora gratefully accepted. Using his support, she pushed herself to her feet, wincing at the pain in her bruised ribs.

"I clearly have a lot to learn," she admitted, not just to her trainer, but to herself.

***

The day's training had been gruelling, pushing Kora to the very limits of her endurance. Despite Sophie and Bane quietly rooting for her from the sidelines, their encouraging words and subtle nods providing a small amount of comfort, Kora had only managed two victories out of seven attempts. Every bout had been a test of strength as much as skill, each of her sparring partners seasoned warriors with years of experience etched into every scar and callus. Kora had given her all, but more often than not, she found herself disarmed or pinned to the ground, tasting dirt and defeat.

Back in their tavern room, as night fell, Kora eased herself onto her bed, her muscles protesting with every movement. The rough wool of the blanket scratched against her skin, but she was too exhausted to even pull it aside.

Sophie sat beside her, concern on her face as she surveyed the damage. Gently, she began to murmur healing incantations, her voice a soothing melody as she tended to the worst of Kora's bruises. Although grateful, as her mind whirled with worries, Kora forced a smile she didn't feel.

"You seem grumpy," Sophie observed softly. "What's wrong?"

Kora sighed, her gaze wandering around the cosy room. Paintings of serene landscapes adorned the wooden walls – rolling fields, dense forests, and the occasional seascape. The fire in the hearth crackled warmly, casting flickering shadows that played across the paintings, bringing the tranquil scenes to life with shifting light and shadow.

"I wish I'd done better," Kora finally admitted, a tinge of shame in her tone.

"Are you kidding?" Sophie said immediately, clearly saddened by Kora's self-doubt. "This kind of training takes time. Relying solely on natural talent won't be enough against a powerful wizard. Ideally, we'd have years to prepare, but we're working with what we've got. I'm making sure to read up on all the tricks and magic that we might find ourselves up against, and I'm still struggling to grasp it, let alone put it into practice. We're learning together, Kora. It's ok that we're not perfect right away. Besides, for what it's worth, I thought you were incredible out there."

Kora blinked, a slow smile spreading across her face as Sophie's words sank in.

"I hadn't thought of it that way," she confessed. "I've been so focused on how much I want to save everyone... It's frustrating to realise it'll take time."

"We need to do this the right way, not the fast way," Sophie insisted. "Wizards are incredibly powerful. If we rush in unprepared, we're doomed – and so is everyone we want to save. No one becomes a master of anything overnight."

"Sophie's right," said Bane from his bed of blankets in the corner, looking up from the bone he'd been gnawing on. "We should all try to get some sleep. Exhaustion does nobody any good. I had to endure a lot of that when I was held against my will by those goblins."

Kora, Sophie, and Bane each settled on their respective beds, appreciating the comforting warmth from the fireplace. The gentle glow of the flames created a soothing ambiance, helping them to relax.

"Goodnight, Sophie," Kora said softly, her voice filled with gratitude. "Thank you for your words."

"Goodnight, Kora," Sophie replied with a gentle smile. "We'll get stronger together. Rest well."

"Goodnight, both of you," said Bane. "We'll be ready for whatever comes next."

"Goodnight, Bane," Kora and Sophie said in unison, their spirits lifted by the bond they all shared.

As the room grew quiet, the trio drifted off to sleep, their hearts fortified by the support and camaraderie they had found in one another.

Chapter Seven

Weeks later, each day had been filled with gruelling training and hard-won progress. Now, as the sun hung low in the sky, casting long shadows across the practice field, Kora faced her final test. At the far end of the expanse of trampled grass stood a figure that commanded attention – a necromancer. Despite his role as a generous volunteer in her training, his stark presence was a chilling reminder of the evil Kora sought to vanquish back in Northfox.

The necromancer belied the sinister nature of his craft. Barely in his mid-twenties, he cut a striking figure, with snow-white hair cascading down his back and facial features that would be considered handsome in different circumstances. When his lips twisted into a knowing smirk, it hinted at the darkness lurking beneath the surface.

At his side, a small army of skeletons stood to attention, their bleached bones clattering softly in the breeze. Empty eye sockets stared blankly ahead, awaiting their master's command. With a single clawed finger, the necromancer pointed at Kora, and chaos erupted. The skeletons lurched forward, their movements jerky yet driven by an unnatural malice.

Kora sprang into action, her muscles in peak condition after weeks of intense preparation. As the skeletons closed in, one of them raked their bony fingers across her cheek, leaving a series of shallow cuts.

In one fluid motion, Kora jumped back to put some distance between herself and the skeletons. She quickly drew her training bow, nocking and releasing an arrow with breathtaking speed. The air sang with the passage of the projectile, which found its mark with precision. The arrow struck the neck bone of the nearest skeleton, causing its skull to topple to the ground with a hollow thud.

Twisting to avoid another bony swipe, Kora aimed low, targeting the spine of another skeleton. The arrow found its mark, and the creature's lower half crumpled, leaving it clawing ineffectively at the earth. Meanwhile, a particularly fast-moving skeleton advanced, its twin daggers flashing as it charged furiously towards Kora.

A deafening crack split the air, accompanied by a flash of inky darkness. The blast of dark magic splattered harmlessly against an invisible barrier mere inches away from where Kora stood. Her heart leapt into her throat as she realised how close she'd come to being struck by the necromancer's spell.

"Thank you, Sophie!" she called out, relieved that her friend's protective magic had saved her once again.

Refocusing on the immediate threat, Kora fired more arrows, shattering the remaining few skeletons into a pile of lifeless bones.

With the skeletons defeated, Kora turned her attention to her main opponent. The necromancer's hands wove complex patterns in the air, conjuring orbs of writhing black and red miasma. The projectiles moved with an eerie, otherworldly grace, pulsating with malevolent energy as they hurtled through the air towards Kora. Each orb seemed to defy the laws of nature, its motion fluid and unnervingly precise, as though guided by a dark, unseen force.

Gritting her teeth, Kora dodged two of the spectral missiles. A third hurtled towards her, only to dissipate against Sophie's magical shield. From the corner of her eye, Kora saw her friend's face contorted in concentration as she struggled to maintain the protective barrier.

"Ugh!" Sophie grunted, her frustration evident as the shield flickered and wavered under the assault.

Knowing she had to end this quickly, Kora took careful aim. Time seemed to slow as she released her arrow, watching it arc gracefully through the air. With a satisfying thud, it struck the padding on the left side of the necromancer's chest. He gracefully raised his hands to signal defeat.

Kora lowered her bow and approached the necromancer with a steady stride. Extending her hand in a gesture of respect, she offered a firm handshake. The necromancer, his expression reflecting admiration and acceptance, clasped her hand firmly in return.

"Thanks for sparring with me," Kora said with a warm smile. "You almost had me there."

"You're welcome," he said. "I didn't go easy on you."

His gaze shifted to Sophie, who was approaching.

"You were phenomenal," he told her before standing back to address them both. "I wish you the best of luck in your upcoming battle against the wizard. You've shown tremendous skill and determination today. May your courage and wisdom guide you."

After parting ways with the necromancer, Kora and Sophie began their walk back to the tavern. The setting sun painted the sky in brilliant hues of orange and pink, a beautiful backdrop to their conversation.

"Everyone in Whimsville has been so good to us," Sophie mused. "I'm going to miss it when we leave."

"I agree," said Kora. "We've both learnt more in these past few weeks than I ever thought possible, and I know Bane has too."

"He's definitely earned his rest today," Sophie said with a soft chuckle. "He put his all into that training session against that goblin. It would be easy to think he holds a personal grudge against all goblins, but I think he's more driven by his desire to fight alongside us."

As the two women continued along the cobblestones towards the tavern, a sense of bittersweet anticipation hung in the air. The quaint buildings, adorned with flickering lanterns, seemed to whisper their farewells.

Entering the tavern, Kora and Sophie ascended the worn wooden staircase. They entered their room to find Bane curled up on his bed in the corner, the subtle rhythm of his breathing offering a comforting presence as they settled in.

Once everyone was in their respective beds, Kora lay awake for a while before finally succumbing to sleep. Her mind raced with not only strategies and contingencies, but a burning need to defeat Wizard Wygor and restore the town of Northfox to its former glory.

92

Chapter Eight

The sun dipped below the horizon, painting the sky in hues of deep crimson and purple as Kora, Sophie, and Bane approached the decaying town of Northfox. For days, they had travelled along the dirt road, an unsettling sensation of being watched dogging their every step. Now, as they entered the town proper, the feeling intensified.

Bane's obsidian fur bristled, his amber eyes darting from shadow to shadow as he padded alongside his companions. His muscles were coiled tight, ready to spring into action at a moment's notice. Kora's elven senses were on high alert, her keen eyes scanning the dilapidated buildings that loomed on either side of the road.

The stench of decomposition was overwhelming, a miasma of rot and despair that seemed to cling to everything. Beneath their feet, the ground was a patchwork of dark, crumbling earth and cracked cobblestones. As they ventured deeper into Northfox, the true extent of its desolation became apparent.

A grim tableau presented itself: the skeletal remains of a horse, its bleached bones scattered among the splintered wreckage of a wagon. Houses sagged on their foundations, windows gaping like eyeless sockets. And from every shadow, every darkened doorway, eyes gleamed – some filled with terror, others burning with an unholy crimson light.

As night fully descended, the sky groaned, heavy with the promise of rain. Suddenly, Kora's breath caught in her throat. There, in the shadows between two crumbling buildings – a flash of movement, unnaturally quick.

"By the gods!" Sophie exclaimed in horror. "What was that?"

There was no time for answers. The streets erupted into chaos.

Pale, emaciated forms crawled from the darkness on all fours, their humanity twisted into something monstrous. Jaws hung open, revealing rows of needle-sharp teeth that clacked together with a sound like rattling bones. Fingers had elongated into wicked claws, and their eyes – jet-black save for their eerie red glow – fixed upon the trio with predatory intent.

"They're everywhere!" Kora shouted, quickly moving to fire arrows as fast as she could nock them.

Bane snarled at her side, hackles raised. Shapes lunged from every shadow, moving with terrifying speed.

"Kora, behind you!" Sophie screamed.

The sheer force of the enemy behind Kora knocked her onto her knees. Pain exploded across her back as razor-sharp teeth tore into her flesh, causing her to cry out.

Bane moved instantly, his jaws clamping down on Kora's attacker as he savagely shook the creature, tearing it away with fervour.

Through the shock of it all, Kora could hear Sophie nearby, her voice rising as she frantically recited an arcane chant. Warmth flooded through Kora as Sophie's healing magic took hold. The bleeding stopped, but a smarting sensation remained.

"Thanks," Kora said, her voice raspy as she forced herself back on her feet.

The relentless onslaught continued, waves of monstrosities crashing against the desperate trio. Kora's quiver emptied at an alarming rate, each arrow finding its mark with deadly precision.

"I'm running low!" she shouted over the cacophony.

Sophie's voice cracked with exhaustion as she chanted, her magic a thin barrier between the cursed and their annihilation.

"We can't... keep this up... much longer!" she said desperately.

Bane's fur was matted with blood – both his own and that of their enemies. His jaws snapped shut on another attacker, bones crunching beneath his strength.

The rain fell hard, turning the street into a muddy quagmire. Kora's boots slipped as she dodged a lunging creature, its claws raking through the air.

In trying to avoid the relentless onslaught, Sophie struggled with her own footing, her spell faltering for a crucial moment.

"Tread carefully!" Kora warned, turning to fire another arrow into the fray.

Just when it seemed that the tide of monsters might overwhelm them, a new figure descended from the storm-wracked sky. Clearly a wizard, he floated down on tendrils of dark magic. His beard was a tangled mess, his skin pale and drawn tight over his bones. When he smiled, it revealed teeth as sharp as those of his monstrous creations.

"Well, well," he said, his voice crackling with malicious glee. "If it isn't the exile, returned to the town that cast her out. Tell me, Kora, why come back to a place that so blatantly doesn't want you?"

Kora's eyes blazed with fury as she fixed her gaze on the wizard. Rain streamed down her face, mingling with blood and sweat.

"You!" she said, her voice ringing out clear and strong as she raised her bow to aim at his heart. "I know what you've done, you snake!"

"I don't know what you're talking about, elf," the wizard said nonchalantly, his face twisting into a sneer.

"Don't lie to me, Wizard Wygor!" Kora shouted, her words cutting through the chaos around them. "You told the townsfolk that I was the one who cursed them. You poisoned them against me! And when they doubted your lies, when they questioned you, you forced their hand, didn't you?"

The wizard let out a small laugh, his response chillingly indifferent.

"You're the source of this corruption," Kora continued, her voice dropping dangerously low. "You're the reason Northfox is on its knees!"

"Perhaps we can reach an agreement," the wizard mused lazily, stroking his ragged beard. "I'll spare five towns of your choosing if you simply turn and walk away. I have important work here, you see, and I'd hate for it to be interrupted."

Without hesitation, Kora fired an arrow. As it sped towards the wizard's chest, he swiftly waved his hand and muttered indistinguishable words, summoning a shimmering shield that deflected the projectile. The arrow fell to the ground, looking insignificant and pathetic as it clattered harmlessly against the earth.

"I sense your weapon is designed to hit its mark," he said, unconcerned. "What a pity that my defences make you no match for me."

The wizard withdrew a wand from the depths of his robes. Faster than lightning, Sophie conjured a radiant force field, its iridescent surface pulsing with arcane energy. Kora seized the fleeting moment of distraction. In one fluid motion, she nocked an arrow, drew her bow taut, and released.

The projectile sang through the air, a harbinger of pain, finding its mark with unerring precision. It pierced the wizard's hand, eliciting a howl that echoed above the low rumble of thunder. The wand clattered to the ground, a symbol of power now rendered impotent.

Agony seemed to course through the wizard's veins, his injured hand a throbbing beacon of weakness. Desperation contorted his features as he raised his other arm, trembling fingers grasping at invisible threads of power. But his magic, once a torrent, now sputtered like a dying flame. Each feeble attempt to summon his arcane might was met with failure, his concentration shattered by the arrow protruding grotesquely from his flesh.

Kora stood resolute, her eyes locked onto her target. She nocked her bow again, every muscle in her body trembling with tension. The string creaked under the strain, a low note of impending doom. As she held her breath, time itself seemed to slow, the world narrowing to this singular, decisive moment.

When she finally released the arrow, it was as if the very fabric of reality bent to her will. The projectile glowed an otherworldly green, cutting through the air with a purpose that transcended mere physical laws. It flew straight and true, an emerald comet streaking towards its destined impact.

In that eternal instant, the arrow found its mark, striking the wizard's skull with a sickening sound: the crunch of bone giving way, a wet squelch of violated flesh, a whistling of displaced air. Dark blood erupted in a macabre fountain, temporarily obscuring the wizard's agonised expression.

The wizard's eyes, once filled with malevolent power, now widened in shock and disbelief. His mouth gaped, attempting to form words that would never be spoken. As if in slow motion, his limbs began to slacken like strings being cut from a puppet. The light of life in his gaze flickered into nothing, finally extinguished.

With a hollow, reverberating thud, the wizard's body crumpled to the ground. The fall of this tyrant, this scourge upon the land, was unceremonious in its finality. No grand explosions, no earth-shattering cataclysms – just the dull impact of lifeless flesh meeting unyielding stone.

As the echo of the wizard's fall faded, Kora's battle-honed senses remained alert. Her eyes, still burning with the intensity of her final shot, swept across the street. What she saw made her breath catch in her throat.

Where grotesque abominations had raged just moments ago, there were now figures both familiar and strange. The transformation rippled outwards from the wizard's corpse like a stone cast into still water. Monstrous flesh melted away, revealing the true forms beneath.

Humans emerged from the twisted shapes of various creatures – some weeping with joy, others standing in stunned silence as they rediscovered their humanity. An orc blinked in confusion, staring at his hands as if seeing them for the first time in years. A goblin fell to her knees, overwhelmed by the sudden return of her own mind and body.

Among the faces, Kora noticed a familiar woman approaching, her steps hesitant and her eyes downcast. This woman had been part of the mob that had chased Kora out of Northfox, but now her demeanour was vastly different.

"Kora," the woman began, her voice trembling. "We owe you an apology. That monster, that Wizard Wygor, he threatened to turn us all into those creatures if we didn't do as he said. We were weak, and afraid, and we took it out on you. Can you ever forgive us?"

Kora's mind raced, memories of her exile warring with her desire to help.

"I understand," she said after a thoughtful pause.

"We're so sorry," the woman's husband said, stepping forward with a look of shame. "By the time we realised the wizard was responsible for the curse and had falsely blamed you, he had the entire town at his mercy. We couldn't protest. We were terrified."

"It will take time for the hurt to fade," Kora said softly, "but I forgive you all. We have all suffered at the hands of evil. Now, let's work together to rebuild Northfox, and to honour those we've lost."

As a feeling of relief settled over the town, some residents began the process of clearing the debris. However, their moment of peace was short-lived. The storm above intensified, lightning arcing across the sky in unnatural patterns. A shadow passed overhead –

something large and looming with leathery wings.

Bane, his ears perking up and his nose twitching, growled low in his throat. His hackles rose, and he took a step closer to Kora, his eyes fixed on the sky.

"I don't like the look of that," he said warily.

"Wizard Bargot?" Kora uttered in disbelief, the words falling out of her mouth as she recognised the newcomer.

The familiar figure descended from the tempest, a smug grin plastered across his face. His dragon, with its crimson wings beating powerfully, took off into the stormy sky, leaving the scene as quickly as they had arrived.

"Excellent work, my dear Kora!" Wizard Bargot crowed, gesturing to Wizard Wygor's corpse. "You've done precisely as I hoped you would. With that fool out of the way, Northfox is now ripe for the taking!"

Kora, Sophie, and Bane exchanged worried glances, their expressions reflecting the unease that had settled over the town. Around them, everyone stood frozen in fear, their initial relief giving way to anxiety as murmurs of dread filled the air.

Wizard Bargot's laughter echoed through the ruined streets, a sound of pure malevolence.

"My unwitting pawns," he said to the trio, "your reward shall be a quick death. After all, I am nothing if not merciful."

Kora's heart sank as she realised the true depth of the betrayal: she had been set up to vanquish one evil only to pave the way for another, who was potentially an even greater threat.

Chapter Nine

The air crackled with violent energy as Wizard Bargot's true nature revealed itself. In a horrifying instant, the bow he'd given Kora melted away in her hands like quicksilver. Her eyes widened in disbelief, her fingers grasping at empty air where her weapon had been moments before.

Before Kora had time to process the loss, the sky above erupted in a dazzling, terrifying display. A bolt of lightning, impossibly bright and moving with unnatural speed, lanced down from the rumbling clouds. As it advanced, a shimmering force field sprang to life around her. The lightning ricocheted off the magical barrier, saving her from what would surely have been a fatal blow. Despite this protection, disorientation caused Kora's legs to give out beneath her. She collapsed to her knees, her chest heaving as every nerve in her body screamed in protest.

Tears streamed down Kora's face as she covered her eyes, momentarily blinded by the overbearing light. Whimpers of terror escaped her lips, a sound so raw and vulnerable it was almost lost in the chaos of the storm. The world around her seemed to melt and warp, reality bending under the strain of Wizard Bargot's dark magic.

For a moment, despair threatened to overwhelm her. But then, images flashed through her mind: families in this town and beyond, innocents who would suffer if she failed. With a grunt of determination, Kora fought to stand up, forcing her eyes open to face her traitorous foe.

Wizard Bargot stood before her, a cruel smirk twisting his features. He tilted his head mockingly, gesturing with an outstretched hand for Kora to approach.

Through the haze, Kora felt a familiar warmth spreading through her body. Sophie, her face etched with concentration, stood nearby, her hands glowing with a soft, healing light. The magic began to counteract the dizzying effects of the lightning, grounding Kora and restoring her balance.

"Hang in there, Kora!" Sophie called, her voice cutting through the confusion. "I've got you!"

With her senses restored and her focus rejuvenated, Kora felt a surge of righteous anger coursing through her. She threw back her head and let loose a battle cry, a sound of defiance in the face of the overwhelming odds.

Wizard Bargot's eyes narrowed, his amusement giving way to genuine concern.

"Impressive," he said with a snarl, raising a now-clawed hand to the turbulent sky. "But it counts for nothing. The music of the storm will shatter your ears and your body!"

True to his word, each lightning strike now carried with it an eerie, soul-piercing sound that reverberated through the air. Bane, displaying remarkable agility, narrowly avoided a bolt that threatened to split him in two.

The wolf was unwilling to let the wizard win. With a mighty leap enhanced by Sophie's magic, Bane soared higher than should have been possible. His powerful jaws clamped down on the wizard's ankle, his teeth sinking into the tyrant's flesh and bone. Wizard Bargot's scream of pain and surprise cut through the storm's cacophony as he was violently yanked back to earth.

Seizing the opportunity, Sophie unleashed an arc of fire from her hands. It streaked through the air, slamming into Wizard Bargot and setting his robes ablaze. He howled in agony, only for the storm above to answer his call. A sheet of rain pelted down, extinguishing the flames but leaving him battered and vulnerable.

Enraged, the wizard thrust his hand towards Bane, tendrils of electricity spinning from his fingertips. The attack hit the wolf in the face, sending him into violent convulsions before he collapsed, motionless, to the muddy ground.

"No!" Kora and Sophie cried out in unison at the sight of their fallen companion.

Grief and fury warred within Kora as she grappled with the limitations of her ability to stop such a formidable enemy. Sophie, too, was visibly weakening, her shoulders slumping with exhaustion.

It was in this moment of despair that hope arrived from an unexpected source. A rough tap on Kora's shoulder drew her attention to an orc, his expression stoic. In his hands, he held a simple bow and quiver of arrows.

"They're not enchanted, nor are they magical," he said gruffly. "But they might just be your best option."

Gratitude welled up in Kora as she accepted the weaponry, quickly slinging the quiver over her shoulder. As she nocked an arrow, her eyes locked with Wizard Bargot's. He sneered with contempt.

"I don't need that weaponry you gave me," Kora said sharply, her voice dripping with disdain. "My aim is pretty decent on its own, thank you very much. It always has been."

What followed was a deadly dance of attack and evasion. Kora released arrow after arrow, each one narrowly missing as Wizard Bargot demonstrated surprising agility for his age. The muddy ground beneath Kora's feet threatened to betray her at every turn, making each shot a challenge.

Then, from behind Kora, an unexpected projectile sailed through the air – a large boulder. Kora wasn't alone in her fight: she had the whole town behind her. The heavy rock struck the wizard squarely in the forehead, momentarily throwing him off balance. A trickle of blood ran down his face, and in that instant of distraction, Kora saw her chance.

Time seemed to slow as she drew back the bowstring for another shot. Her eyes narrowed in concentration, every fibre of her being focused on this single, crucial moment. With a whispered prayer, she let the arrow fly.

The projectile streaked through the air, a beacon of hope in the storm-wracked night. It struck true, burying itself deep in the wizard's chest. His eyes widened in shock and disbelief as the magic of the storm began to turn against him.

The roiling clouds above seemed to collapse inward, funnelling down into his body.

Thunder roared one final time, and then, in an instant, the sky cleared. Stars twinkled overhead, a stark contrast to the chaos that had reigned moments before.

For a heartbeat, Wizard Bargot was still as a statue. Then, like a felled tree, he toppled forward, crashing face-first into the muddy earth and shattered cobblestones.

A collective gasp rose from everyone present. It was quickly followed by tentative cheers, but Kora knew the ordeal was far from over. Dropping her borrowed bow, she rushed to Bane's side, her heart pounding with fear. Sophie was already there, tears streaming down her face as they knelt beside their fallen companion. There was no sign of life: no heartbeat, no breathing.

"There must be something we can do," Kora pleaded, her voice cracking with emotion.

"Step aside," Sophie commanded, her face set with determination. "Let me try something."

Kora complied and watched anxiously as Sophie began to administer chest compressions, her hands glowing with a soft blue aura. The magic flowed into Bane, working in tandem with the physical resuscitation efforts. After what felt like an eternity, Sophie leaned in, breathing directly into Bane's muzzle.

For a moment, there was nothing. Then, miraculously, Bane's chest began to rise and fall. His breathing was shallow at first, but soon developed into full-bodied gasps. His legs twitched spasmodically, as if trying to run from an unseen threat.

"Shh, Bane," Sophie soothed, her voice heavy with exhaustion. "You're safe now. Breathe. Don't try to do too much. Focus on remaining stable."

Relief washed over Kora as she watched Bane slowly come around.

As the three friends shared a moment of calm and camaraderie, the townsfolk began to approach them.

"Thank you, brave heroes," an elderly orc said emotionally, his head bowed in humble gratitude.

Before any of the appreciative trio could respond, a shadow passed overhead. Then, with an earth-shaking thud, an enormous dragon landed before them, its crimson scales glinting in the starlight. Kora tensed, fearing another battle.

Chapter Ten

As the dragon settled, Kora saw something unexpected in its eyes – not rage or malice, but a profound weariness tinged with hope. Although most of the dragon's scales were an intense, shimmering ruby, there were patches where the lustre had dulled, and scars marred its otherwise magnificent form.

"Brave warriors," the dragon announced, his voice deep and resonant as he addressed Kora, Sophie, and Bane, "you have my eternal gratitude for vanquishing the evil Wizard Bargot."

Kora's tension melted away to be replaced by a wave of relief that left her feeling almost giddy. Sophie lowered her hands, the glow at her fingertips fading. Bane sat back on his haunches, his ears twitching with curiosity rather than fear.

"For too long, I was forced to exist in squalid conditions and participate in Wizard Bargot's vile schemes," the dragon continued, his tone softening. "You have liberated not only this town and all the other dwellings that evil old man had his eye on, but myself as well."

Kora's thoughts churned with regret. It made her so sad to think that the dragon had endured such a horrible time under the ownership of Wizard Bargot. In the flurry of everything else that had been going on, she had never stopped to question the dragon's welfare. She had always viewed the dragon as part of her enemy, a compliant cohort within the monstrous force to be reckoned with, never considering the possibility that it too was a victim. The thought of the dragon being forced to serve the wizard, stripped of its freedom and dignity, filled her with a deep disappointment. It was a noble creature, deserving of respect and compassion, not the mindless beast she had imagined.

"I'm so sorry," Kora said to the dragon. "I didn't realise you were under such duress. If I'd have known, I could have..."

"It's ok," the dragon interrupted, not a hint of

disappointment in his voice. "You weren't to know. Wizard Bargot was always a master of his façade. I'm glad that he is no more. Anyway... one good thing to come out of my time with him is that I was able to see into the same crystal ball he used to keep watch over you. I have been able to observe the three of you on your journey, and I have words for each of you."

Turning to Bane, the dragon's eyes glimmered with warmth.

"Noble wolf, your loyalty and companionship are a testament to the strength of your spirit. Know that you are cherished by Kora and Sophie. Never again will you face the loneliness of a packless existence."

Breathing a deep sigh, Bane tilted his head, clearly moved by the dragon's words. Sophie stood straighter as the dragon turned to address her next.

"Young lady, your magical prowess grows daily. Continue to learn, continue to practice, and the world will open countless doors for you."

"Thank you," Sophie murmured in awe, her eyes shimmering with pride.

Finally, the dragon's eyes met Kora's, prompting her to feel a surge of emotions – pride, relief, and a deep, abiding sense of belonging.

"Kora," he said, "you are a true hero. Your dedication and integrity have forged unbreakable bonds with your companions. You've saved Northfox. The townsfolk will forever be in your debt. You will always be welcome here. Fear not the spectre of exile – your strength and skill in defeating both wizards has proven your sincerity and bravery beyond doubt."

Kora felt tears prick at the corners of her eyes. She had been through so much, the sting of accusation hurting her to her very core, and now, she could hold her head high in the town she had always called home.

"Remember my words," the dragon said as he addressed the townsfolk. "You are incredibly lucky to have someone like Kora on your side. May you never doubt her again."

The townsfolk stood in stunned silence as the dragon's words resonated through the square. Eyes that had once glanced at Kora with suspicion and doubt had softened into blended expressions of shame and admiration. Murmurs rippled through the crowd, people exchanging guilty glances, their faces reflecting a collective realisation of their unjust treatment of the elven woman.

As the dragon watched approvingly, the townsfolk began to gather around Kora, offering words of gratitude and pledges of support. Kora felt the weight of their sincerity, the sting of past accusations fading as the warmth of their newfound respect enveloped her. She stood taller, her heart swelling with the sense of belonging and acceptance she had longed for.

"Now then," said the dragon, drawing everyone's attention back to him as the first rays of dawn painted the sky in hues of pink and gold. "I shall help you all in rebuilding this town. I will call upon my kin to assist. It will be a joy to reunite with my clan, free from the shackles of servitude. After the evil I was forced to participate in, helping to restore your home is the least I can do."

Epilogue

I n the months following the defeat of the two evil wizards, the town of Northfox slowly began to rehabilitate, rising from the ashes of its cursed past.

The rebuilding efforts were arduous. The townsfolk worked tirelessly, but many tasks proved too challenging – even for their combined strength. True to his word, the dragon played a pivotal role. He dedicated himself to repairing the damage done to Northfox. His large form moved with surprising grace, lifting heavy stones and reconstructing buildings with the help of his powerful kin. With his newfound freedom, the dragon had managed to summon his clan from far away, their combined strength proving to be a formidable force in the reconstruction efforts. Together, they transformed the town's skyline, erecting structures that would have otherwise been impossible to re-establish so swiftly.

Despite the physical rebuilding of Northfox, the emotional wounds left by the curse ran deep. Many townsfolk remained in mourning for the lives lost. Among them was Sophie, who continued to grapple with the loss of her parents. The curse had not just taken homes, but had shattered families and disrupted lives. The pain of such loss was a shadow that lingered over Northfox, and only time would serve to heal those wounds.

Aid came from the village of Whimsville. Its residents arrived with wagons full of supplies, offering food and materials to help Northfox recover from the devastation of the curse, which had destroyed crops and livestock. Kora, Sophie, and Bane were heartened to reconnect with the familiar faces from Whimsville. They learned that the tavern and shop there were thriving, no longer burdened by the black market that had flourished under the fear of wizard attacks.

Proud that his teachings had served the trio well, the burly orc Melvin was particularly pleased to see Kora, Sophie, and Bane. He extended an open invitation to the residents of Northfox, offering his training grounds for self-defence and confidence-building. The dragons, too, offered their services, promising to ferry anyone who wished to visit Whimsville on their broad backs.

Despite having been blamed for the curse and driven from Northfox, Kora held no grudges against anyone. Instead, she chose to embrace forgiveness and understanding. The townsfolk, in turn, took the experience as a crucial lesson. They vowed never again to judge so hastily, recognising that the potential to wield magic did not equate to malevolence. This newfound wisdom fostered a sense of unity and resilience within the town.

The three heroes decided to remain in Northfox, committed to safeguarding their home. Kora, Sophie, and Bane had found a place where they belonged, a town that now revered them not only as saviours, but as integral residents. To honour their bravery and dedication, a statue bearing their likeness was erected in the town square. It stood as a testament to their courage, and a reminder of the strength found in unity and forgiveness.

Under the watchful gaze of Kora, Sophie, and Bane, Northfox had been given a chance to heal. The scars of the past were still visible, but with each passing day, the town grew stronger. The laughter of children returned to the streets, merchants reopened their shops, and the fields began to yield crops once more. Northfox, once a place of despair, began to transform into a symbol of resilience and hope, forever grateful to the unlikely trio who had fought to save it.